Gordon's
House

Written and Illustrated by
JULIE BRINCKLOE

Doubleday & Company, Inc., Garden City, New York

Library of Congress Cataloging in Publication Data

Brinckloe, Julie.
  Gordon's house.

  SUMMARY: Five stories featuring the antics of Gordon the bear and his animal
friends.
  [1. Animals—Fiction] I. Title
PZ7.B7685Gq   [E]
ISBN 0-385-06886-7   Trade
ISBN 0-385-06905-7   Prebound
Library of Congress Catalog Card Number 75-33189

CONTENTS

For
Mr. Amery

GORDON'S HOUSE

I am going to Gordon's house.
You can come with me
if you want to.
We might make cocoa
and sit by the fire,
or walk in the woods,
or do almost anything.

Come along, don't be shy.
Gordon is really very nice . . .
and I know he will like you.

GORDON THE TREE

HOW TO ATTRACT BIRDS: Make believe you are a tree.

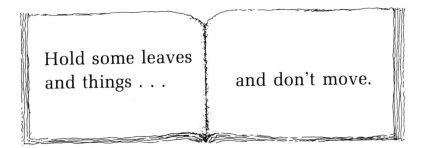

Hold some leaves
and things . . .   and don't move.

If a bird lands
on your head . . .   don't move.

If she puts
sticks and grass
on your head . . .

don't move.

And when it gets
dark and she sits
on your head . . .   be very still . . .

she's sleeping.　　　　The end.

 # THE BABOON GAME

Gordon and Edith were sitting on a log.
"What shall we do?" said Edith.

"I don't know," said Gordon.
"Just sit here, I guess."

"No," said Edith, "we'll play a game.
I'll make believe I'm something.
You guess what it is."

Edith thought of a baboon.

She walked back and forth
with her wings drooping.

"Are you a kite with no wind?"
said Gordon.
"No," said Edith. "Guess again."

She hopped around
and made grunting sounds.

"Are you a great big rabbit
with a cold?" said Gordon.
"No," said Edith. "Guess again."

She hung from a tree
and scratched her feathers.

"Are you a leaf with fleas?"
said Gordon.
"An apple with worms?
Are you a broken branch
with ants in its pants?"

"No, no, no," said Edith.
"I'm a baboon!"

"Oh," said Gordon.
"What's a baboon?"

GORDON AND THE HOPPY THING

Gordon was eating an ice cream cone
when a bug hopped by.

"What are you eating?" said the bug.
"Ice cream," said Gordon. "Have a lick."

The bug took a lick of ice cream.
It tasted so good that
he wanted the whole cone
for himself.

And he thought of
a way to get it.

"Hey, there," said the bug.

"Can you hop?"

"Yes," said Gordon. "I can hop."

"Can you hop over sticks?"
said the bug.

"Sticks are easy,"
said Gordon.

"Can you hop over stones?" said the bug.

"Yes," said Gordon.
"I can hop over
stones, too."

"Well, then," said the bug.
"Can you hop over me?"

"Of course I can," said Gordon.
"You are just a tiny little bug."

"I'll bet you my *cap* you can't,"
said the bug.

"I'll bet you my *cone* I can,"
said Gordon.

Gordon tried to hop over the bug.
But the bug was hopping, too.
Gordon hopped after him.

They hopped over sticks.

They hopped over stones.

They even hopped
over a stream.

But Gordon could not hop over that bug.
"All right, hoppy thing,"
he said finally.
"You win my ice cream cone."

The bug took
Gordon's cone.
He looked inside.
The ice cream was gone!
It had all dripped out the bottom.

"My ice cream!" he cried.
"It's all melted away!"

The bug sat on a rock and grumbled,

and Gordon hopped over him
                                just
                                    like
                                        that.

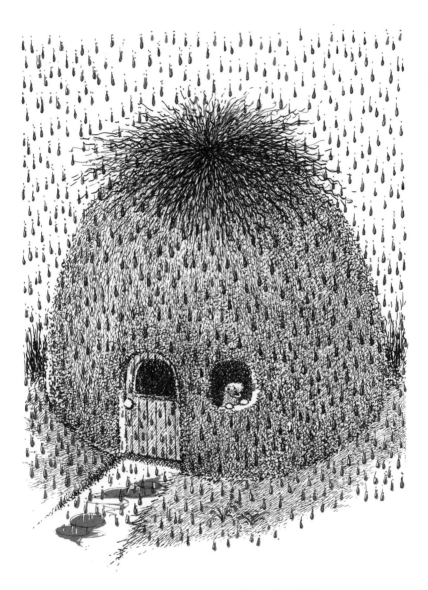

ONE RAINING DAY

"What a lovely day," said Gordon.
"I think I'll paint the rain."

"Hi, Gordon," said Marvin.

"What are you painting?"

"Rain," sighed Gordon.

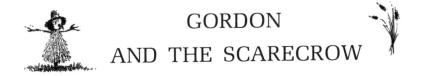

GORDON
AND THE SCARECROW

Gordon saw a scarecrow in a bean patch.
"Hello," said Gordon.

The scarecrow didn't answer.

Gordon leaned on the garden wall.
"Hey, you. Hello," he said.

The scarecrow didn't answer.

Gordon climbed into the garden.

"Why won't you talk?"
he said.
"Do you have a cold?"

The scarecrow didn't answer.

"Are you sad?" said Gordon.
"Are you tired of standing
in the bean patch all day?
Do you want to play with me?"

The scarecrow didn't answer.

"You don't like me, do you?"
said Gordon.
"You don't want to talk to me.
But I'll *make* you talk.

I'll pick a bean from your garden."

Gordon picked
the biggest bean
he could find.

"Aren't you going
to holler?" he said
to the scarecrow.

The scarecrow didn't answer.

So Gordon ate the bean.

"I ate your bean," he said.
"Hey, scarecrow, I ate your bean."

The scarecrow didn't answer.

Gordon looked at the scarecrow
and scratched his head.

"I don't think you *can* talk," he said.
"You're just an old heap of straw
with no feelings at all."

All at once Gordon felt silly
standing in the bean patch
He climbed over the garden wall.

"So long, you old heap of straw," he said.

"So long," said the scarecrow.

JULIE BRINCKLOE was born in Mare Island, California. She studied art at Sweet Briar College and received a bachelor of fine arts degree from Carnegie-Mellon University in 1972. Ms. Brinckloe has illustrated many stories and poems including *The Bollo Caper* by Art Buchwald and *Dirty Dinky and Other Creatures: Poems for Children* by Theodore Roethke, and is the author-illustrator of *The Spider Web* and *Gordon Goes Camping*. She now lives in Pittsburgh, where she teaches art to young people, while continuing her career as a writer and illustrator.